MY ROBOT'S GONE WILD

ILLUSTRATED BY

DAVE COUSINS CATALINA ECHEVERRI

LITTLE TIGER

LONDON

In memory of my grandad Ivor Davies, who believed you could do, or build, anything if you put your mind to it! – DC

To Sofi and Abi, who always find a way to make me smile – CE

STRIPES PUBLISHING LIMITED
An imprint of the Little Tiger Group
1 Coda Studios, 189 Munster Road,
London SW6 6AW

A paperback original
First published in Great Britain in 2021

Text copyright © Dave Cousins, 2021
Illustrations copyright © Catalina Echeverri, 2021

ISBN: 978-1-78895-183-8

CHAPTER 1

ALL CHANGE

"A ROBOT!" I said. "From *Star Wars.*"

The train guard frowned. "Oh, I thought you were the Tin Man!"

My sister laughed. Jess was dressed as Gru from the film *Despicable Me.* (She thinks villains are more fun!) Her best friend, Ivana, made the costume, which was cheating as far as I was concerned. I'd done mine all on my own. If Robin had still been living with us, he could have helped and it would have looked a million times better. But then everything would be

1

better if Robin came home.

The guard cast a glance round the carriage. "I've never seen so many strange costumes on one train!"

"Everyone's going to Comic Con," Ali told her. "People dress up as their favourite characters from films and stuff."

"It's nice your gran dressed up too.
She looks more like a robot than you do!"
Ivana gave a nervous laugh. "Yes, you like
dressing up, don't you, Grandma?"
The old lady nodded.
"Affirmative!"
"Ha! I see what she did
there! Very robotic." The guard
chuckled and handed back our
tickets, then turned to the group
of Pokémon sitting behind us.
"That was close!" said Jess.
The thing is, our 'gran'
– dressed up like a robot –
was ACTUALLY A ROBOT
dressed up to look like our
gran! Our *real* grandma was
in Scotland, hiding out with
Robin, who is also a robot…
I should probably explain.

3

Grandma is an inventor. She made Robin as a babysitter for me and Jess, but then TV Celebrity Fleur Pickles found out what the robot could do and tried to copy him. Unfortunately, the robots *she* made were dangerous and we had to destroy them. Fleur Pickles swore revenge – so Robin and Grandma went into hiding with Granny Anderson. We suspected that Ms Pickles had people watching us – which is why we were pretending to go to Comic Con, when really we were catching a train to Scotland to visit them.

The robot on the train with us was made by our neighbour, Mr Burton. He was the first person to try and steal Robin's secrets … but that's another story!

Mum and Dad didn't want us to travel all the way to Scotland alone, so RoboGran was here to look after us. We also had our dog,

Digby – but he was more likely to run and hide at the first sign of trouble.

"What ARE you doing?" My sister stared at Ali.

My best friend was peering through an enormous pair of binoculars. "A woman over there keeps looking at us!"

"Probably because you're pointing giant binoculars at her!" said Jess.

Ali shrugged and lowered the glasses, but I knew what he was thinking – any one of these people could be a spy for Fleur Pickles.

We got off the train with the Comic Con crowd, then ducked into the toilets to change.

It turns out station cubicles are NOT a good place to try and extract yourself from a cardboard C-3PO costume. Apart from the smell and lack of space, I wished I hadn't been quite as enthusiastic with the parcel tape. It took so long we had to run to catch our next train and only just made it. But before I sat down I saw something that made my heart kick.

"It's that woman! The one who was watching us on the other train. She's sitting at the end of the carriage!"

"You think she's following us?" Ali reached for his binoculars.

Jess groaned. "If you two want to play spies, you can go and sit somewhere else. It's embarrassing!" Then she frowned at my friend. "I thought you were changing OUT of your disguise, not putting on a different one!" It was only then that I noticed Ali was wearing a new jacket – it was bright yellow, shiny and slightly too big for him. "Oh, and by the way – your hair's sticking up."

"It's deliberate!" Ali sounded hurt. "It's my new hairstyle."

I didn't realize Ali had an *old* hairstyle. He'd always had the kind of hair that just *sat there* on top of his head. Since when did my best mate care about stuff like hair and clothes?

"I don't know why you dressed up," I said. "You do know we're going camping, right?"

Ali shrugged and glanced at Ivana. SURELY NOT! I knew Ali *liked* Ivana … but there was NO WAY he could be doing all this to impress HER … was there?!

"I can't wait to start Year Seven," said Jess, smirking at me. "Primary-school kids are so childish!"

I stared at her. Sometimes it was hard to believe we were related – let alone TWINS!

"They're doing trials for the school football team in the first term!" said Jess.

Ivana grinned. "You're bound to get in!"

"If you don't get yourself sent off first!" I muttered. As well as being the best player at our primary school, my twin sister also held the record for red cards. Impressive, considering she plays in goal!

Jess stuck out her tongue. "At least *I* didn't get myself locked in the toilets on our induction-day visit and have to be rescued!"

"It wasn't my fault the door got stuck!"

That hadn't even been the worst part. We'd had to play a *fun* game of Shipwrecked, so we could *get to know our classmates from other schools*. Well, they'd got to know ME all right. It's hard to forget the kid dangling from a rope for the entire game because he's too scared to let go!

I didn't want to change schools. Hardacre Academy was MASSIVE! There'd be loads of kids from other primary schools too. What if Ali found a new best friend? Someone into hair gel and shiny yellow jackets!

I hated the way everything was changing. Ever since our last day at Northfield Park Primary, life seemed to have speeded up and I wasn't sure I liked it. I was looking forward to seeing Robin. Robots don't suddenly start wearing hair-gel for no reason! You can rely on a robot.

We watched the train chug away and looked around. Nobody else had got off at our station, so at least we weren't being followed.

"Strathwilder," said Ali, reading the rusty sign. "I thought Granny Anderson lived in the Nether Regions?"

Jess frowned. "Granny Anderson lives at Wilder Croft, near Loch Wilder," she said, checking the address Mum had written down for us.

"Affirmative," said RoboGran.

The station was just a bare platform in the middle of a field. Beyond the hedge were more

STRATHWILDER

fields and — in the distance — even more fields,
rising steeply to become mountains. No buildings.
No people. Digby sniffed the air and shivered.

"When Granny Anderson said we were
going to be wild camping, I didn't realize she
meant THIS wild!"

"What's the matter?" said Jess. "Scared
you'll get eaten by a grizzly bear?"

"They have BEARS in Scotland?" Ali
looked worried.

"I think it's beautiful," said Ivana. "So peaceful."

Almost immediately that peace was broken by a strange yet familiar sound echoing round the hills – a rough, growling rattle, like some kind of ancient monster in pain.

Digby gave a yelp and hid behind Jess. We all knew what was coming…

WHERE THE WILD
THINGS ARE

The growling stopped. Granny Anderson
stepped off the motorbike and removed her
goggles. "Och! You've been at it again!"

"What?" Jess looked worried.

"Growing!" Our great-grandmother grinned.
"I swear you were just wee when I saw you
last." She held out her arms. "But you're no
too big for a hug."

Granny Anderson is stronger than she looks
– I thought my ribs were going to crack! But
I was more worried about the close proximity

of my face to the furry creature curled round her neck like a scarf. As usual, Wee Freddie was fast asleep, but that didn't reduce the impact of the ferrety aroma as my nose was pushed into his fur.

"Where's Robin?" I asked.

"There wouldnae been room in the sidecar," said Granny Anderson, hefting our bags into the shed-on-wheels attached to her motorbike.

Even with RoboGran riding behind Granny Anderson, there was barely room for the four of us, our luggage and Digby. But that was the least of our worries.

Granny Anderson drives *FAST*. She only uses her brakes in an emergency, which meant our journey over the winding mountain pass was TERRIFYING.

We bounced along the narrow track, hurtling round corners with only a rickety fence between us and a sheer drop into oblivion. I tried closing my eyes, but that was even worse – darkness filled with the demonic howl of the engine and the rattling, groaning protests of the shed-on-wheels.

Just when I thought it would never end, Granny Anderson yanked the brake and we skidded to a halt next to a tiny stone cottage.

"Thank you for flying Anderson Airways," said Granny Anderson, chuckling. "You may unfasten your seat belts."

"Would you like a cup of tea?" said RoboGran to nobody in particular. Then her head rotated in a complete circle and she repeated the question.

"I reckon that ride shook up her circuits," said Ali, wobbling as he stepped out of the sidecar.

Granny Anderson peered at the robot. "Maybe we'd best switch her off for now. We'll get your grandma to have a look at her later!"

"Where *is* Grandma?" asked Jess, looking around.

I'd thought Grandma and Robin would be here to meet us, but there was no sign of them. I couldn't imagine Robin getting on very well in a place like this. Everywhere you looked there was just hills, trees and rocks.

"Can I use your toilet?" said Ali. "I really ne— ARGHHH!" My friend let out a shriek and dived BACK INSIDE the shed-on-wheels. "Over there!" he shouted. "LOOK!"

The creature standing by the gate was huge and round with short, furry legs. Its body was covered in shaggy, rust-coloured hair.

Granny Anderson laughed.

"Och! It's just one of ma lassies come t'say hello!"

"Lassies! Aren't they bulls with horns like that?" said Jess.

Our great-gran shook her head. "It's no just the menfolk that have horns wi' beasties."

"Beasties?" Ivana frowned.

"That's what we call 'em." Granny Anderson walked over and scratched the cow behind the ear. "They're awful friendly. Just watch oot for the horns!"

The cow nudged Ivana with its nose, then nibbled at her jacket.

"It's trying to eat Ivana!" said Ali. "Somebody HELP HER!"

"Och, she's just checkin' to see if you've any food!" Our great-gran gave the beastie an apple. "Why don't I show you where you'll be camping?"

But Ali wouldn't move until the cow had been herded to a safe distance.

We grabbed our stuff from the shed-on-

wheels and followed Granny Anderson down
the hill towards a bank of trees. It was dark
inside and the air smelled damp.

"Aye, watch your step," she warned
as my foot sank into a puddle of liquid
mud. "You're in the wild now!"

I felt the icy water
squelching between my toes
and decided I didn't like the
wild – there was far too much
nature involved!

"This is Loch Wilder," said Granny
Anderson as we emerged on to the banks of a
wide lake glistening in the late-afternoon sun.

"Wow!" said Ali. "Our own private beach!"

Jess and Ivana dropped their bags and ran
across the pebbles to where a small wooden
jetty jutted out over the water.

"Can we go swimming later?" my sister
asked, her eyes wide with excitement.

"If you can stand the cold, aye. Don't go too far oot, mind – it's awful deep. Bottomless some say!"

"That's impossible!" said Ali.

The old lady's eyes sparkled. "You're in the wilds o' Scotland now, laddie. There's all sorts here that folk'll tell you is impossible, and yet…" She shrugged. "You see that white smoke there, slitherin' across the water? Folk around here believe that's dragon's breath!"

"Isn't it just mist?" said Jess.

"Aye, probably." Granny Anderson gave me a wink. "Though it could be the water dragon…"

"The WHAT?" My sister's eyebrows disappeared under her fringe.

"Legend has it there's a fire-breathin' water dragon livin' doon there!"

"Have you ever seen it?" asked Ali, his expression a mixture of excitement and fear.

"My da claimed he saw it once, but he was one for the tall tale, right enough. Ma always said it was *more dram than dragon!*" She chuckled.

For a moment nobody said anything. We stared at the ghostly mist drifting across the loch. Then the sun went behind a cloud and a sudden breeze rippled the surface of the water.

Camping had sounded like fun. But now we were actually here in the wilderness, next to the dark wood and the lake with the sea monster ... I wasn't so sure.

Digby was inspecting the camp. There were so many new smells the dog didn't know where to start. He'd been dashing all over the place, but suddenly he stopped and barked at a clump of bushes.

"Looks like he's found something!" said Ali.

"Can't be anything scary or he'd have run away," I pointed out, feeling a shiver of doubt creep over me.

Then one of the bushes moved.

And I don't mean it shook in the wind.

I mean, it STOOD UP and walked towards us.

Which is when me and Ali jumped a metre in the air – and ran!

"ROBIN!" said Jess.

Even in my panicked state, I remember thinking, *Robin's here! He'll save us!*

But, when I turned round, I saw that Robin WAS the bush!

"I was testing my new camouflage," said the robot, removing a layer of leaves. "I'm sorry if I frightened you."

"What do you need camouflage for?" I asked, wondering why he couldn't have just said *hello* like a normal person.

"I am learning to survive in the wild," said Robin. "Your grandma has provided me with a number of upgrades to help. My new feet have caterpillar tracks – look!"

"Wow!" said Ali.

The robot had new hands too. His little finger unscrewed to reveal a sharp blade, while his thumb and middle finger were a flint set, so all he had to do to spark a fire was click his fingers!

Even without his camouflage, the robot looked very different to the Robin we had waved off from the school car park just a few months ago. His smart suit and wig had been replaced by an army-style shirt and shorts – he even had a bandana wrapped round his head!

"He's gone wild!" I whispered to Ali.

"I know! Cool, isn't it?"

I wasn't so sure. I liked the old Robin – the one who enjoyed baking cakes and playing *Revenge of the Robots*. This *wild-man* upgrade was all wrong. I wanted MY robot back!

A UNIQUE GIFT FOR
DESTRUCTION

Ali pointed at the two bundles on the ground.
"What are those?"

"Your tents," said Robin.

"Aren't they a bit small?"

Granny Anderson laughed. "They pop up!
Totally Automatic Self-pitching Tents!"

"You mean ... Grandma made these?"

Grandma's inventions often sounded
great at the idea stage ... unfortunately they
didn't always work quite as intended. The
AUTOMATIC PORRIDGE MACHINE for

example – it was designed to serve breakfast, but had turned out to be a lethal weapon!

"Are they safe?" I asked.

Robin stroked his beard. "We experienced a few technical difficulties to begin with, but there's nothing to worry about now."

"What kind of *difficulties*?"

"One of the sleep pods kept going into *automatic pack-up mode*," said the robot. "Fortunately nobody was inside at the time."

"What would have happened if they had been?" Ivana asked.

"They'd have been turned into origami!" said Ali, looking worried.

"Master Jake." Robin pointed to the nearest bundle. "This one is for you and Master Ali. Simply pull the red ring to initiate pitching sequence."

"Don't let Jake do it!" said Jess. "It'll probably explode!"

I scowled at my sister, but I knew what she meant. Things had a habit of falling apart in my hands. Dad said I had *a unique gift for destruction.*

But I wanted to get our tent up so me and Ali could zip ourselves inside – away from all this NATURE! We could play *GamePad* and maybe then Ali would stop acting weird.

I took a step towards the bundle and noticed everyone else casually backing away. It was a tent. How wrong could it go?

I grabbed the red ring, took a deep breath … and pulled.

There was a click, followed by a loud hissing as the bundle started to unfold. Digby ran for cover.

"That's a lot of smoke!" said Jess as the pod began to grow, flapping like a giant bird.

"It's from the jets that make it pop up," the robot explained.

"Is it supposed to hover above the ground like that?" asked Ali.

Robin stroked his beard. "The jets will stop firing momentarily."

But they didn't. The tent was now two metres above the ground and rising, its guy ropes trailing like kite tails.

"Oh, dear," said the robot. He grabbed one of the ropes, but the jets continued to fire, lifting him into the air.

"Quick!" shouted Jess. "Grab his legs!"

I jumped but Robin was already too high.

Ali tried, but neither he nor Ivana could reach either.

Jess pushed past me, running at full pelt, and launched herself at the dangling robot.

All that goalkeeping must have helped because she caught him!

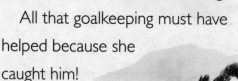

But then the wind picked up and both of them started drifting down the beach towards the loch.

We ran over and grabbed my sister's legs, trying to stop the tent from towing Robin AND Jess out across the water.

"I don't know how much longer I can hold on!" said Jess.

"Let go!" Robin called down. "Save yourselves!"

"NO!" I shouted. Granny Anderson had said the loch was bottomless. IF ROBIN FELL IN, WE'D LOSE HIM FOREVER!

Then something grey and sticky flew through the air and *thwacked* into the tent.

"Hold 'im steady!" called Granny Anderson, hobbling towards us with the **AUTOMATIC PORRIDGE MACHINE** in her hands.
"I need to take oot those jets!" She fired again and the pull of the tent lessened. Another shot and we were able to start dragging Jess and Robin away from the loch.

A final clod of porridge was too much for the jets – they spluttered, coughed and finally fell silent. The tent sank to the ground like a deflated balloon.

Of course the other tent popped up perfectly.

"The jets must've been faulty on Jake's one," said Granny Anderson. "We'll get your grandma to have a look when she gets here. Wouldnae want them going off in the night and takin' you on an unexpected wee flight!"

"I suggest we make sure your guy ropes are secured tightly," said Robin, hammering a peg into the ground, while Digby and Wee Freddie fought over who got to lick the porridge off the tent.

I was staring out across the loch, thinking *I must have done something to it*, when a dark shape broke the surface of the water then disappeared again. It happened so fast, I wasn't sure if I'd imagined it.

"What's up?" said Ali. "Your face has gone all funny."

Jess snorted. "How can you tell?"

I hesitated. They'd laugh – say it was just my imagination and the mist. It was Granny Anderson's fault. Those spooky monster stories…

BUT THERE IT WAS AGAIN!

"Ali! Have you got those binoculars?"

The glasses were so heavy it was impossible to hold them steady, let alone focus. The surface of the loch lurched about like I was on a ship in a storm – one minute I got a close-up of the water, the next sky and clouds. Then something else flashed past – or rather … someONE.

I swung the binoculars back and there it was again – a woman in a red coat on the hill overlooking the loch. She was pointing a long-lens camera directly at us. Suddenly I forgot all about the thing in the water and gasped.

"FLEUR PICKLES!"

"WHAT? Where?" Jess snatched the binoculars from me. "I can't see anything!"

"Are you certain it was TV Celebrity Fleur Pickles, Master Jake?" Robin was scanning the hillside with his super-zoom eyesight, but the woman had vanished.

"It looked like her."

"*Like* her or *was* her?" said Jess.

"I don't know."

But if it *was* Fleur Pickles...

Granny Anderson hobbled over. "Could be rustlers casing the joint."

"Who? Doing what now?" Ali looked confused and scratched his head.

"Rustlers," said Robin in his *reading from the internet* voice. "The name given to criminal gangs who steal livestock, usually cattle or sheep."

"They're after ma beasties! A couple o' my neighbours have been robbed already." Granny Anderson glared up at the hills. "Whoever it is, I'll wager they're up to no good! If it's her off the telly, she'll be after the metal man, right enough."

"She must want Robin REALLY BADLY to have come all this way herself!" said Ali. "What if she's built more evil robots and brought them with her?"

"Or," said Jess, handing the binoculars back, "Jake's just imagining things – AS USUAL!"

"I have an idea," said Ivana. "We could ask Brett to check if Ms Pickles is at her factory. If she is there, then we'll know it can't be her who's watching us."

"Brett?!" Ali was frowning.

"You think it's a bad idea?"

"I didn't know you and Brett were friends, that's all…" Ali had an odd expression on his face. It was probably because Brett Burton had been mean to me and Ali since Reception. It was only in the last few months that he'd stopped hassling us.

Ivana blushed. "He's actually quite nice when you get to know him."

"But how can we contact him?" I asked.

"He's my friend on FaceChat," said Ivana.

Which is when Ali screamed.

I understood he might be jealous, but it was a bit of an extreme reaction! Then I realized that my friend wasn't looking at Ivana.

I turned and saw a dragon emerge from the loch. The water was bubbling and hissing around it, cloaking the creature in clouds of steam as its head swung towards us, flames spouting from its gaping jaws.

THE THING FROM
THE DEEP

"WATER DRAGON!" said Ali in a strangled croak.

Digby flashed past us, heading for the safety of the trees. I wanted to follow, but my legs seemed to have stopped working. I hoped one of Robin's survival upgrades included *self-defence against dragons*.

"Hang on a minute!" said Jess. "That's a submarine!"

"Disguised to *look* like a water dragon!" Ivana laughed.

"GRANDMA!" we all said together.

Sure enough, as the *water-dragon-submarine* crunched on to the beach, we could see a familiar face grinning at us through the window.

The submarine looked like it was made from an old car with an upside-down bathtub bolted to the roof. Its long neck was a string of tin cans, dripping with water and bits of seaweed.

The car spluttered to a halt and Grandma climbed out, flapping over to us in a wetsuit and flippers.

"Sorry I wasn't here to meet you," she said, giving us a soggy hug. "The sub needed another test run so I thought I'd surprise you!"

"You did that all right!" Ivana told her. "But what's it for?"

"It's our secret weapon against them cow-rustlers I was tellin' you aboot!" said Granny Anderson, helping Robin and Grandma push the submarine out of sight among the trees.

Ali frowned. "How is a submarine going to stop someone stealing the cows? Are you going to hide them in a secret underwater base?"

Jess gave a loud sigh.

"Not exactly," said Grandma. "The cows graze in the fields around the loch, so it's hard to keep track of them. But from the water we can see all the way round and reach either bank much faster. Plus the rustlers won't know we're there!"

"So you're going to hide underwater in the

submarine," said Ivana. She pointed to the water dragon's long neck. "Is that a periscope?"

Grandma nodded. "I remembered the old legend of the water dragon and thought it would be a good disguise AND make us scarier!"

"A fire-breathin' monster is a wee bit more intimidatin' than two grannies in an auld mini!" Granny Anderson chuckled.

"Can we have a ride in it?" said Jess.

"You'll have to put your swimming stuff on," said Grandma. "She's not completely watertight."

"Are you sure it's safe?" Ali looked doubtfully at the home-made submarine and Jess gave a snort.

"Don't come if you're scared!"

"I'm not scared! It's just …" I knew what he was thinking – Grandma's pop-up tent had almost sent Robin into space. A lot more could go wrong with a submarine!

"Will we be able to see underwater?"
Ivana asked.

"So long as the wipers don't pack up!"
Grandma grinned. "You'll be amazed at how
many fish there are in the loch – turtles too!"

I shuddered. I don't like water – mainly
because I can't really swim. So going
*under*water in an old car was not top of my list
of FUN THINGS TO DO!

"Or we could stay here and play *Revenge of
the Robots Two*," I suggested.

But Ivana started going on about turtles and
smiling at Ali.

"I might go actually," he said. "I've never
seen a turtle."

I shrugged to hide my disappointment.
"Sure. No problem. I'll stay here. You know …
keep an eye on the camp and that."

"Master Jake and I will finish securing the

sleep pods," said the robot. At least *he* was loyal.

"Right!" said Granny Anderson. "That's me away up to the hoose. Jobs to do and time's no waitin' on me."

I stood on the beach with Robin, while Digby – brave now the water dragon was leaving – ran along the water's edge, barking as the bath-sub slid under the surface and disappeared in a fizz of bubbles.

There was a strange heavy feeling in my chest, but I shrugged it away. "You're going to love the new *Revenge of the Robots* game," I told Robin, leading the way towards the tent. "It's got an option to play as a robot! The console version is better, but we'll have to wait until we get home to play that."

"You must show me next time I come to visit," said Robin.

I stared at him. "What d'you mean? You're

coming back home with us ... aren't you?"

The robot shook his head. "Grandma will be returning with you, but I will stay here. Granny Anderson is *no as young as she was*!" said Robin, using the Scottish accent from his satnav voice processor. "She needs my help to catch the rustlers."

"But what about me ... and Jess? Grandma made you to be OUR babysitter!"

The robot smiled. "You and Miss Jess will be starting secondary school in September. You no longer need a babysitter."

"NO! That's exactly WHY we need you!" I told him. "I'm not ready to go to a new school. How am I supposed to survive Year Seven without you?"

The robot rested a hand on my shoulder. "Your new school seems frightening at the moment because it is unfamiliar. You will soon get used to it."

"But what if I don't?"
I could feel the panic
swarming round me like
a cloud of insects. "You
HAVE to come back!"

"There is also Fleur Pickles," said
Robin. "It is too dangerous for me to return."

"But ... Fleur Pickles might be HERE!"
I wasn't sure if that was good or bad now!
Why was it all so complicated? "I wish things
would just go back to how they were! Why
does everything have to change?"

The robot smiled and handed me a fishing
rod. "Do you not think that life would be dull if
nothing ever changed?"

"No. I'd like it," I said. "What's this for?"

"We are going fishing," said the robot,
leading me towards the jetty.

"FISHING!? Don't you want to see my
new game?"

"You are in Scotland, Master Jake –
surrounded by opportunities for real-life
adventure."

"I think I prefer pretend adventure," I told
him. "It's safer!"

"It is good to try new things," said Robin,
"or you risk missing out on something you
might enjoy. Also, in the wild, the ability
to catch your own food could mean the
difference between life and death!"

I wondered if this was part of Robin's new
wild-man programming – teaching me and Jess
how to survive. There was no point in arguing:
once the robot was on a mission, nothing would
stop him from carrying out his instructions.

The wooden boards of the jetty creaked as
we walked out over the water. "How deep is it
here?!"

"The structure is perfectly safe," said Robin,
opening a plastic box.

"Ugh! WHAT ARE THOSE?"

"Sardines," said the robot. "We will use them as bait to attract the fish."

Digby had followed us on to the jetty and looked excited at the prospect of food, but even he changed his mind when he saw what was in the box.

Once the gruesome stuff was over and our fishing lines were dangling in the water, it wasn't actually that bad. I was happy to be hanging out with Robin again. I started telling him how weirdly Ali was behaving.

"You know he's started wearing HAIR GEL!"

"That *would* explain why his hair is more vertical than usual..." said the robot.

"I don't know what's wrong with him. He doesn't want to do any of the stuff we used to. Like just now – since when was Ali more interested in turtles than video games?"

"Ah!" said Robin. "I believe Master Ali is more interested in Miss Ivana than the turtles."

I almost dropped my fishing rod. "WHAT?"

"I observed Master Ali earlier – his heart rate increases when Miss Ivana is near and he spends a larger proportion of time looking at her than anyone else."

I'd suspected as much, I just hadn't wanted to believe it. Ali had always liked Ivana, but in the past all he'd done was smile at her and go a bit dopey when she was around. It had never got in the way of important stuff! This was taking things to a new level.

"It's perfectly natural, Master Jake," said the

robot. "As you get older, your body changes and you become aware of the opposite sex."

"OK, STOP! Just stop talking! I don't want to hear any more about it!"

"But—"

"NO!"

I was saved from further disturbing conversation by a sudden twitch on my fishing line.

"You've got a bite!" said Robin.

Suddenly I really wanted to catch a fish. The others would be impressed if I actually LANDED ONE while they were just out gawping at them through glass!

"How big do you think it is?" I asked.

"I believe that some of the pike in here are bigger than you!" said Robin.

"Wow! You'd better watch out, Digby!" I laughed, but the fishing rod felt like it had come alive in my hands and I was struggling to hold on. "It's really pulling!"

"The fish will soon tire," said the robot.
"You've got this."

I didn't feel like I'd got it – I felt like IT had
got ME.

"Almost there!" said Robin, ready with the
net.

But, as I tried to reel it in, the fish made
a final bid to escape and I felt myself being
dragged along the jetty like a waterskier.

I hadn't realized just how slippery the boards were. The next thing I knew there was no more jetty under my feet – just air. For a brief moment I was flying.

And then I wasn't.

CHAPTER 5

NOOOOOOOOOOO OOOOO!

The water was so cold I couldn't breathe – I thought I was going to die! Then I felt a hand on my arm, dragging me to the surface, and tasted air again.

"If I'd known you were going swimming, Master Jake, I'd have reminded you to wear your trunks!" said the robot, pulling me back on to the jetty. "I suggest we return to camp and I will light a fire."

I nodded. My teeth were chattering too much to speak, but there was something important I HAD to say.

"We … don't … n-n-need … to … t-t-tell … the others … about this," I spluttered.

Robin nodded. "Of course not, Master Jake. Our secret."

I was in the tent, looking for dry clothes, when I heard the bath-sub return. I quickly pulled a T-shirt over my head and dived back outside so the others wouldn't guess anything had happened.

Ali was helping to push the water dragon back under cover. "I saw a turtle!" he said.

"Which one?"

"Michelangelo, I think."

We exchanged a grin.

Jess pulled off her snorkel. "So what did *you* get up to?"

"Oh, you know … just hanging out with

Robin … doing survival stuff." I pointed to the fire the robot had made while I was changing.

"Why's your T-shirt on inside out?" My sister frowned and a guilty blush flushed my cheeks.

"We went fishing," I said, avoiding the question. "I caught a massive pike!"

Jess looked around. "Where is it then?"

"Um… We had to let it go. It would have broken Robin's fishing rod. You should have seen how much it was bending."

"We did." Jess started to laugh.

"We were watching you through the periscope," said Ali, looking sheepish. "Grandma wanted to test the focus range. We didn't mean to spy."

So they'd seen everything.

"It actually looked kind of cool," he said. "When that fish pulled you off the jetty, you were, like, proper flying through the air!"

"The funniest part was you splashing around in ten centimetres of water like you were drowning," said my sister. "Hilarious!"

"NOOOOOOOOOOOOOOOOO!" Ali's cry echoed round the camp and bounced mournfully off the mountains.

We found him in the tent. "Something got into my bag and ate all my snacks!"

There were chewed clothes and torn chocolate wrappers everywhere, cheese balls scattered across the floor among a pattern of muddy pawprints.

"Mmm," said Robin, whipping out his magnifying glass and slipping into DETECTIVE MODE.

"I deduce that our suspect is approximately twenty-five centimetres in height, has brown hair and messy eating habits. Furthermore…" The robot held up a finger and paused dramatically. "He had an accomplice!"

Jess gave a loud tut. "I could have told you it was Digby and Wee Freddie without a magnifying glass! Serves you right for leaving your tent open."

"I didn't!" said Ali. "I made sure it was closed before we went in the…" Then he stopped and looked at me.

"I'm sorry!" I said. "I must have forgotten to zip up the tent when I heard you coming back."

Ali kept saying it didn't matter, but I could tell he was annoyed.

"Don't worry, Master Ali," said Robin. "I will be cooking something special this evening. Much tastier than crisps and chocolate – if I do say so myself!"

See? That's why I needed the robot around! If anything could save this disaster of a day, it was Robin's legendary apple-and-cinnamon muffins!

I stared at what was in the bowl on my lap. It definitely wasn't an apple-and-cinnamon muffin.

"Hedgerow stew!" said Robin. "Made from locally foraged plants and fish from the loch."

"A proper wild supper," said Grandma, who I noticed wasn't eating with us. She *said* she was too busy trying to fix RoboGran to stop for food...

"Perhaps it'll taste better than it looks," I whispered.

Ali frowned. "I hope so because it *looks* like the Incredible Hulk was sick in my dish!"

I laughed and Ali grinned. Maybe he'd forgiven me.

"This is lovely, Robin," said Ivana. "Thank you!"

Surely she was just being polite?

But NO – Jess and Ivana were ACTUALLY EATING the stuff! Me and Ali exchanged horrified looks.

"You should try it," said Ivana, smiling at Ali.

She could smile all she liked – there's NO WAY Ali was going anywhere near—

I watched in disbelief as my friend dipped his spoon into the bowl. He must REALLY want to impress Ivana.

Ali raised the spoon to his lips – there was a piece of fish perched on a bed of dripping green slop. He hesitated, then…

"Mmm," said Ali. He hated it – I could tell. I wondered how impressed Ivana would be when he spat it out again! Ali swallowed. "That was actually all right," he said, turning to me. "You should try it."

I stared at him, then down at my bowl. Maybe it wasn't as bad as it looked…

My spoon made a squelching sound as I pushed it into the stew. It was a lot like the noise my foot had made when I stepped in that mud puddle earlier.

Perhaps if I closed my eyes it would help? But closing my eyes didn't block the smell.

My stomach gave a lurch. "I'm actually not that hungry," I said.

I might have got away with it if my belly hadn't chosen that moment to let out a loud gurgle of hunger.

As the fire burned down to a mound of glowing embers, the darkness seemed to creep in at the edges of the camp. Back at home there are street lamps so it never gets properly dark. Out here in the wild, there were no streets to *have* lamps – and the night consumed everything.

"Time for bed, I think," said Granny Anderson.

Grandma had deactivated the jets on our tent, but I was still worried that the sleep pod might decide to automatically pack itself up with me and Ali inside!

That wasn't the only thing troubling me.
I had to find a way to persuade Robin to come home with us … if Fleur Pickles didn't get him first. She was probably up in the hills right now, plotting to invade our camp during the night.

Then there was Ali. What was I going to do if he didn't want to be my best friend any more?

There was no way I was going to sleep with all that rattling round my brain. Perhaps some gaming would help? Maybe I could pretend that me and Ali were just having a sleepover at home and that everything was normal again.

"You want to try the new *Revenge of the Robots* game?" I asked as Ali zipped up the tent.

"I'm a bit tired actually," he said, crawling into his sleeping bag. "Maybe tomorrow?"

"Oh … OK." I was glad it was dark so Ali couldn't see my face.

I rolled over and found my book. *Calvin and Hobbes* always makes me laugh, and I was feeling a bit better until I realized I needed the toilet. But Granny Anderson had told us not to go wandering about after dark. I focused on the pages and tried not to think about it.

Then Ali started to snore. He sounded like a piglet trying to blow up a balloon. It was the final straw. How was I supposed to sleep through that!

THE NEW NEW
SECRET WEAPON!

"I TOLD YOU it wasn't Fleur Pickles!" said Jess the next morning at breakfast.

"Brett sent me a message on FaceChat," Ivana explained. "He says he got to speak to Fleur Pickles herself, face to face!"

"How did he manage that?" Ali didn't look happy.

"Brett told the person at reception that he had some important information about a robot!"

"That's actually pretty clever for Brett," said

Jess. "Anyway, Fleur Pickles told him she's not interested in robots any more. She said robots are *totally last year*!"

"How rude!" Robin sounded hurt. "I'd like to make it known that I am very much THIS year!"

After a sleepless night of worry and Ali snoring, my brain was struggling to work out if this was good news or bad. But if Fleur Pickles wasn't interested in robots ... surely that meant it would be safe for Robin to come home again?

That was GREAT news!

Then I remembered the cattle thieves. Robin said Granny Anderson needed his help catching the rustlers. But what if WE caught the rustlers while we were here? Then the robot wouldn't have any reason not to come home with us! Plus, if Grandma got RoboGran working properly, we could leave *her* behind to help Granny Anderson instead!

"HELLO? Moira? Is that you?" Granny Anderson was hobbling round the camp, shouting. It looked like she was talking to herself, but she was actually on the phone. *Hands-free!* she'd told us – very proud of the headset Grandma had made for her.

"A badger, aye!" said Granny Anderson. "That's terrible!" She stabbed the ground with her stick. "Have you tried greasin' it wi' goose fat?" The old lady listened, then laughed. "Hittin' it wi' a hammer usually does the trick!"

"What *is* she talking about?" Ali whispered.

I shrugged. With Granny Anderson, it could be anything.

Finally our great-gran said goodbye and turned to us. "That was my neighbour, Moira. Had six of her beasties stolen last night! Reckon that means we're next!"

"In that case," said Robin, "might I suggest we

continue trials for our new secret weapon?"

"You mean the submarine?" Ali looked excited.

"No, this is a NEW new secret weapon," said Grandma.

"Have you fixed RoboGran? Is SHE the new secret weapon?" This could be my chance to suggest leaving the other robot in Robin's place.

But Grandma shook her head. "I'm afraid RoboGran is going to have to wait. This is something we've been working on for a while. Though our early field tests haven't gone well."

Why didn't that surprise me?

"Um, Granny Anderson?" Ali raised his hand like he was in school. "Why did you tell Moira to hit it with a hammer?"

"Did I?" The old lady frowned in thought. "No, it's gone. Sound advice though. Fixes most things!"

"May I present," said Grandma, "the very latest in anti-cattle rustling measures. I give you … SPY COW!"

A beastie crashed through the trees into the camp and Ali yelped.

But there was something … *odd* about the cow. First it went one way, then the other. Finally it shuffled sideways like a crab, tripped on a guy rope and fell over.

"Another resounding success!" sighed Grandma.

"Is that Robin in there?" Ali asked, when he realized the cow wasn't a real beastie.

Up close, you could see it was a costume – like something from a pantomime, just more robotic. Grandma removed the fake head.

"I'm terribly sorry," said Robin. "This uneven terrain makes it very difficult to maintain my equilibrium."

"You mean you keep falling over?" said Jess.

The robot nodded.

Ali frowned. "How is Robin dressing up like a beastie going to help catch the rustlers?"

"If there's no moon, we cannae see so well from the loch," said Granny Anderson. "We need someone closer to the cows, just in case."

"And if he looks like a beastie the rustlers won't know he's actually a guard robot," I said. "That's clever."

"It works perfectly until he tries to move!" Grandma pulled out a screwdriver and crouched down next to Spy Cow. "The gyroscope might need recalibrating. Or it could be a misaligned grommet."

"You could try hitting it with a hammer!" said Ali, grinning at Granny Anderson.

"Aye, that usually does the trick!"

Grandma gave them a look. "I'll get it to work, it just might take some time."

But time was something we didn't have.

"Could a person fit in there?" I pointed at the cow.

Grandma frowned, then her eyes lit up. "Oh, I see what you mean! If we took the robotics out and just went back to a beastie pantomime cow with people inside... You know, that might actually work!"

"Genius!" said Granny Anderson.

"Me and Ivana will do it!" said Jess.

"Hey! What about me and Ali?"

My sister folded her arms. "YOU TWO?

You'd probably end up walking straight into the loch!"

"But it was MY idea!"

"There's no need to argue," said Grandma. "I made two, so we'd have a backup. You can all have a go."

Granny Anderson chuckled. "You know what they say – two Spy Cows are better than one!"

"I wish you hadn't volunteered us to be a Spy Cow," said Ali, pacing the tent. There wasn't much room, so it looked like he was spinning on the spot. Just watching him was making me feel dizzy.

"I'm sorry! I forgot you didn't like the beasties."

"I do like them. I just … prefer them at a distance. They're scary!"

"Granny Anderson said they wouldn't hurt us."

"Granny Anderson says a lot of things!" Ali frowned. "I don't trust them. You didn't see the way that one looked at me yesterday."

I laughed.

"It's not funny. It's like you being scared of water. I love swimming but you hate it. If you're scared of something, it doesn't matter how anyone else feels about it."

I hadn't thought about it like that. If Ali asked me to go in a boat on the loch, there's no way I'd do it. Being a Spy Cow was like that for him. I really needed to catch the rustlers, but maybe it wasn't fair to ask him.

"We don't have to do it if you don't want to."

Ali looked at me, then shook his head. "No. I want to help. But maybe we don't have to get too close?"

"Definitely!" I said. "Don't forget we'll be in disguise. The cows will just think we're another beastie. They probably won't even notice us."

Ali gave a doubtful nod and crawled into his sleeping bag. Granny Anderson had told us to have a nap because we were likely to be up all night. I closed my eyes, but I was too excited to sleep.

The next thing I knew I was being woken up by a talking tree telling us it was time to go.

"Why are you camouflaged?" I asked the robot, who was covered in branches.

"I will be co-ordinating our surveillance teams from up on the hill, disguised as a pine tree," he told me. "My optical sensors can detect body heat. If the rustlers come, I will be able to see them."

"What do you need us for then?" said Ali.

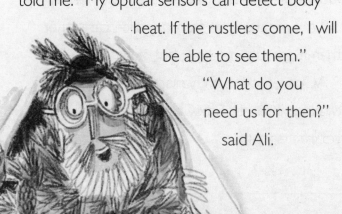

"Unfortunately my sensors only pick up a heat signature. It could be a rustler, but it might also be a rabbit, or a deer, or a beastie! That's where you come in. If I spot any suspicious activity, I will direct the nearest Spy Cow to investigate. Once we have confirmation that the thieves are here, I can call in the water dragon!"

The sky was filled with stars. A full moon hung over the hills, sending a silvery stripe across the loch. I shivered and reminded myself we were going on a stake-out – like cops did on TV. How cool was that? Admittedly they usually did their stake-outs from a police car rather than a pantomime cow, but still.

"Good luck," said Ivana, smiling at Ali as we climbed into our Spy Cow costumes. "I think you're very brave."

"Brave!?" said Jess, her voice muffled by the fake beastie head she was wearing.

Ivana nodded. "Ali is afraid of cows but he's going into the field anyway. That is brave."

I hadn't seen Ali smile so widely since he completed the final boss level in *Revenge of the Robots*!

Robin handed each team a walkie-talkie. "In times like this," he said, "I believe a few words of motivation can help calm nerves and strengthen resolve. If I may?"

"Aye, knock yerself oot," said Granny Anderson.

The robot frowned and we explained that it was just an expression – Granny Anderson didn't actually want Robin to knock himself unconscious.

I wondered what the robot was going to say. I guessed he'd been researching motivational speeches on the internet.

Robin cleared his throat. "Here we go!" he said. "Here we go. Here we go."

"Isn't that a football chant?" whispered Ali.

"Here we go, here we go, here we go – oh!" said the robot, his voice filled with emotion. "Here we go … here we go … here we go. Here we go – oh …" He paused dramatically and cast his eyes round the group

gathered on the beach in the moonlight.

"Here … WE … GO!"

"Well!" said Granny Anderson. "That's me motivated, right enough!"

Robin's beard twitched as he smiled.

STEAK OUT!

Jess and Ivana's Spy Cow headed for the eastern shore, while me and Ali went west. Granny Anderson and Grandma were lying in wait underwater in the bath-sub, and Digby had gone up the hill with Robin. Wee Freddie was roaming about somewhere. Granny Anderson had explained that the ferret would lend a paw and some teeth if required. Either that or he'd find somewhere to curl up and go to sleep.

I was beginning to regret letting Ali be the front of our beastie. As the rear end, I had to bend forwards and hold on to his waist. It was uncomfortable and all I could see was the back of Ali's trousers.

"Hey! No farting!" I told him.

Ali gave a nervous laugh. "I'll try, but you know how I get when I'm frightened."

Not being able to see where you're going is scary. I had to trust Ali and follow where he led, hoping we wouldn't end up in a ditch, or worse! When he stopped suddenly, I bashed right into the back of him.

"What's wrong?" I fumbled for the walkie-talkie. Grandma had told us that if we saw the rustlers we had to radio Robin and scarper. The thieves were dangerous criminals and she didn't want us getting hurt.

"They've seen us!" said Ali, his voice filled with fear.

"THE RUSTLERS!?"

"No! THE COWS!"

"ALI! You scared the life out of me!"

"I'm STILL scared!"

"Sorry! Just ... try to relax and ... act like a cow? Pretend you're eating some grass."

"I can't."

"Why not?"

"I'm too scared to move."

"OK ... just stand still then."

I felt something large bump up against us. Ali let out a whimper.

"She's just being friendly," I told him.

"I don't want to be its friend!"

The cow gave us a noisy sniff, then decided we weren't that interesting and wandered off. Ali started to breathe again.

Suddenly the walkie-talkie squawked, making us both jump. "Red Bull to Rusty Rejects, are you receiving, dummies? Over." It was my sister's voice.

"You're the dummy," I said, clicking the

button to talk back.

"Have you seen anything?" asked Jess. "It's freezing out here and we're bored."

"Nothing happening here either, but we found some cows."

Jess snorted. "Wow! Well done! You two are on fire tonight!"

"Shut up! We're only supposed to use the radio if we see something," I reminded her.

Jess laughed. "OK, losers. Over and out!"

"Jake?" Ali sounded worried again. Perhaps the cow had come back? Or maybe this time it *was* the rustlers!

"Do you think if I asked Ivana to be my girlfriend she might say *yes*?"

I wasn't expecting that.

I didn't know what to say … except, "What do you want a girlfriend for?"

"I like Ivana," he said. "I thought it might be nice to … you know … do things together."

"You mean like … kissing and stuff?"

"NO! Though that might be nice, I suppose.
I mean just … going to see a film or something."

"I'll go and see a film with you. There's that
new superhero one coming out."

"Yeah, Ivana said she'd like to see that."

"Oh, right. I see." And I could. My future
stretched ahead of me, bleak and Ali-free.
My ex-best friend and Ivana sitting together
at lunchtime, walking home after school. Ali
wouldn't want to come round any more. He'd
be too busy with Ivana, holding hands and
deciding what film they were going to see
next. I'd have to go to the cinema with Dad
and he'd fall asleep and start snoring.

"So," said Ali, interrupting my nightmare
vision, "do you think she'd say *yes*?"

This was my chance to talk him out of it.
I was his best friend – he trusted me. If I said
I thought she'd say *no*, he might give up on the

whole idea and I'd get my mate back again.

But I was his best friend – he trusted me. It was obvious Ivana liked Ali. Of course she was going to say YES.

"Robin thinks I should ask her," said Ali.

"Robin? Our robot babysitter Robin?"

"We don't know any other Robins."

"True," I said. "I'm just shocked you asked a robot for dating advice, rather than, say ... your BEST FRIEND."

"I'm asking you now, aren't I?"

"Only after you already spoke to Robin."

Ali went quiet.

"So what did he say?"

"Robin said I should buy some flowers and take Ivana to a romantic place, then get down on one knee and propose. He said I should take a ring too."

"PROPOSE!" I spluttered. "You do know that means asking her to MARRY YOU!? THAT'S why you don't ask a robot for advice on girls!"

"Oh," said Ali. "There aren't any shops around here anyway, so I couldn't get a ring. I did pick some flowers, but Robin said they were poisonous. I think I might wait until sunset on the beach by the loch. Robin said I should say something nice about her eyes first and then ask her."

"About HER EYES!" I snorted. "Like what? *Oh, Ivana, your eyes are so round and you have two of them. Please be my girlfriend!* Something like that?"

"That's why I didn't ask you first!"

There was a noise from nearby.

"Was that a cow?" said Ali.

"Um … I don't think cows can laugh," I said, glancing down at the walkie-talkie. "Jess? You can hear us, can't you?"

"Loud and clear!"

Ali made a strange noise.

"You shouldn't be listening to our private conversation!" I shouted.

"Don't broadcast it on the walkie-talkie then!"

"I didn't realize it was still on. You should have said something."

"What? And miss that! No way!"

I switched off the radio.

"JAKE!"

"I know, I'm sorry!" At least now Ali didn't have to ask Ivana because I'D DONE IT FOR HIM! In fact, I'd probably just helped bring the two of them together and lost my best friend in the process! "I didn't realize the talk button was still—"

"SHUT UP!" Wow! He must be really mad. "Jake, THERE'S SOMEONE HERE!"

"What?" With the shock of what had just happened, I'd briefly forgotten why we were there.

"There's a person on the other side of that wall."

"Is it the rustlers?"

"Who else would it be?" hissed Ali. "Call it in!"

I jabbed the button on the walkie-talkie. "Rusty Rebel to Optimus Pine. Someone's here!"

The robot's voice came back straight away. "What is your location, Rusty Rebel?"

"Um..." It was at times like this that not being able to see anything except the back of Ali's trousers was a real problem.

"They're behind the wall. By the tree!" Ali shouted, which didn't really help as there were trees and walls all over the place.

"Don't worry, we have you in the periscope," said Granny Anderson from inside the bath-sub. "Setting an intercept course. Please clear the area!"

It's hard to run when you're bent over and can't see where you're going. We'd only gone a few metres when I tripped and fell. The sound of tearing Velcro filled the air as Spy Cow separated, its front legs and head shooting off into the darkness.

I rolled over in time to see the water dragon erupt from the loch in a boiling frenzy of steam, fire belching from its jaws.

The cows scattered in fear, but the figure Ali had spotted didn't run. I recognized the woman in the red coat, as she crouched down and filmed the monster rolling up the bank towards her.

It was only when the water dragon stopped
and two pensioners in wetsuits jumped out,
that she stood up and looked like she might
not want to be there any more.

The scene was illuminated by the bath-sub's
headlights and the woman looked round like

she couldn't quite believe what she was seeing.
"Who ARE you people?" she asked the scuba-
diving grannies and rear end of a beastie.

"The question is WHO ARE YOU, lassie?"
said Granny Anderson. "And what are you
doing wi' ma cows in the middle of the night?"

The woman sitting at Granny Anderson's kitchen table didn't look much like a cow rustler.

"We know who you are and what you're doing," said Robin, shining Granny Anderson's table lamp into her face. "There's no point denying it!"

"Oh, OK!" The woman had gone very pale.

"We want the names and whereabouts of your accomplices," said the robot, in full INTERROGATION MODE. "We know you have a hideout so I suggest you tell us where it is."

"I'm here on my own actually," said the woman. "I don't have a hideout, but I can tell you where my tent is."

"We're no as daft as we look, lassie," said Granny Anderson. "You expect us to believe you're thievin' cattle by yerself?"

"Stealing cattle?" The woman looked confused. "I just wanted to get some pictures of the water dragon. I'm writing a book about Scottish legends and came to do some research. I happened to see … that thing you built … in the water, but I didn't get a picture. I've been watching out for it ever since. When I saw your camp by the loch, I thought you were here for the dragon too!"

"You mean you weren't trying to steal Granny Anderson's beasties?" I wanted so much for us to have caught one of the rustling gang, but the woman stared at me as though I'd just suggested she was an alien and demanded to know where she'd parked her spaceship.

"Nice try, lassie!" Granny Anderson leaned across the table. "But, if you dinnae stop messin' us aboot, I'll have to introduce you to Wee Freddie. Trust me – you dinnae want that!"

The woman's eyes widened. "Who's Wee Freddie?"

I glanced across the kitchen to where the ferret was curled up asleep on top of the heater.

Granny Anderson gave a menacing smile. "Tell us what we want to know and you'll no have to find oot!"

"But I'm telling the truth, I promise!" The woman reached into her bag. "Here's one of my books. There's a picture of me on the back. Look!"

Granny Anderson peered at the cover. "Elaine Foster," she read. "Looks like you, right enough."

"My scans suggest the subject is telling the truth," said Robin. "Her heart rate is steady and she has displayed no detectable signs of lying."

Elaine Foster stared at the robot dressed as a tree as though she didn't trust her eyes.

Granny Anderson sat back and told her about the rustlers.

"That's terrible," she said.

"Sorry if we gave you a fright," said Grandma. "And sorry it wasn't a real water dragon!"

Elaine Foster laughed. "This might be a better story anyway!"

Not for me, I thought. Not only had we failed to catch the rustlers, but thanks to my inability to operate a walkie-talkie Ali and Ivana were now officially a couple! All through the interrogation they'd been sitting in the corner, holding hands and smiling at each other.

The night had been a complete disaster. Little did I know that things were about to get a whole lot worse.

CHAPTER 8

A WEE BIT
O' RUSTLIN'

"It looks like we're down to one Spy Cow
for tonight then," said Grandma, examining
what was left of the costume me and Ali
had managed to wreck during the previous
evening's excitement.

"You two jokers can use ours," said Jess.
"Ivana's ankle's swollen up like a football!" Ivana
had tripped and twisted her ankle on the way
back to camp in the dark.

"Master Ali might also be unavailable," said
Robin. "His exact words to me were ... *I'm*

never going anywhere near those cows again!"

After I fell over and our Spy Cow split in two, Ali had kept running. When he finally realized I was no longer attached, he'd turned back and found a dozen terrified beasties stampeding towards him out of the darkness. The cows had been scared by the water dragon, but Ali thought they were chasing him. He'd thrown off his beastie head and run all the way back to the croft where we'd found him hiding in the shed-on-wheels.

"But what if the real rustlers come tonight?" I said.

"May I suggest that you and Miss Jess operate the remaining Spy Cow?" said Robin. "Miss Ivana and Master Ali could monitor the eastern shore from the bird hide."

"Grand idea, Metal Man!" Granny Anderson clapped her hands.

"Hang on a minute," said Jess. "Me and

JAKE? In the SAME cow costume!"

"It's the logical solution to our predicament,"
Robin pointed out.

Jess folded her arms and
scowled. "I don't care
how LOGICAL it is! I am
NOT spending all night
in THAT, with HIM!"

I wasn't exactly thrilled
by the idea either. "Let me talk to Ali."

But it was no use.

"I'm sorry, Jake. I tried, but I just can't do it."
Ali's face was serious. "Anyway, I need to look
after Ivana now she's hurt her ankle."

There was no point trying to persuade him.
The old Ali – my best friend for as long as I
could remember – was gone. Which meant
that catching the rustlers so Robin could come
home was now even more important. If the
only way to do that was to spend the night as

one half of a pantomime cow with my sister —
that's what I'd do.

Clouds gathered over the mountains during
the afternoon. By night-time, they had
formed a blanket, shutting out the stars and
blocking the moon. I'd never seen darkness so
complete — not that it made much difference
to me in the rear end of the cow.

"This is impossible," muttered Jess, stamping
across the hillside. "I can't see a thing! Even if
the rustlers do come, we won't be able to see
them!"

"That's why Granny Anderson thinks they'll
come tonight," I reminded her. "It's a fine
night for a wee bit o' rustlin'!" I said in my best
Scottish accent.

"Optimus Pine to Red Bull." Robin's voice
crackled from the walkie-talkie. "I have you

on my heat sensor."

I pressed the button to reply. "We can't see anything at all. You'll have to guide us. Over."

"There's a group of cows just ahead of you," said the robot. "Continue on your current trajectory and you should make contact any moment now."

"Ow!" said Jess, making contact with a beastie in the dark.

"I think we've found them," I reported. My sister stopped so suddenly I slammed into the back of her.

"Watch where you're going, idiot!"

"How can I? I'm just following you!"

The walkie-talkie squeaked again. "Eagle Nest to Red Bull, come in, please. Over!"

"Hi, Ali."

"You're supposed to say Red Bull receiving."
His voice sounded very near, but really he
was on the other side of the loch, no doubt
cuddled up with Ivana in their cosy bird hide.

I sighed. "Red Bull receiving."

"Anything to report?"

"If there was anything to report, we'd have
reported it!" my sister growled.

"OK, well ... be careful out there," said Ali.

"I don't know what Ivana sees in him," Jess
muttered.

I was about to argue, when I thought, *NO
– why should I defend Ali?* He'd abandoned me
to hang out with his new girlfriend, while I had
to stumble around, dressed as a cow, with my
sister. "Bet they're sitting there, holding hands
and smiling at each other!" I said, checking I
hadn't left the walkie-talkie on again.

Jess grunted, which was as close as she ever

got to agreeing with me.

"Ivana will be telling him how much she likes his jacket! AND his stupid hair gel!" My chest felt weird — like there was a weight pressing down on it. I'd had the same feeling when Grandma and Robin left for Scotland.

"Optimus Pine to Red Bull." The robot sounded excited. "I have multiple heat signatures heading your way."

Was this it? Were the rustlers really coming?

"It's probably just more cows," said Jess.

"Approaching from the west," Robin whispered. "Five metres and closing. You should have visual contact any moment now."

"It's too dark! I can't see ANYTHING!" I could feel Jess swinging the Spy Cow's head round, trying to spot who, or what, was coming.

It was horrible not being able to look for myself. What if the rustlers were sneaking up on us from behind? I strained my ears to listen, but it was hard to hear anything above my own galloping heart.

"Remember," said Robin, "as soon as you are able to give visual confirmation that the rustlers are attacking, you must retreat with the utmost urgency!"

"Roger that!" I muttered, then to Jess, "Can you see them yet?"

"NO! I told you – it's too dark!"

"I have them in your exact location now," said Robin. "Right in front of you!"

"Hang on! I think I can see a light!" Jess whispered.

Unless the beasties had started carrying torches – this was it!

"Red Bull to Optimus Pine!" I hissed. "It's the rustlers. They're here!"

"Good work, Red Bull," said Robin. "I will relay the intercept location to the submarine. Now get out of there!"

I tapped Jess on the back. "GO!" But my
sister didn't move. "What's wrong? We need
to get out of here."

"I'm trying!" said Jess. "There are cows in
the way!"

The moment she said it, I felt the weight of
heavy beastie bodies pushing against us. The
arrival of the rustlers had spooked the cows
who were mooing in alarm. I could hear the
thieves too – their voices sounded close and
seemed to be coming from all around.

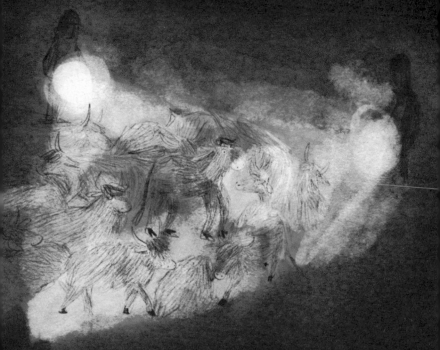

"Get the gate!"

"Drive 'em straight on tae the wagon!"

We began to move forwards, caught in the flow of beasties being herded towards a lorry.

"I can't steer us out!" I could feel my sister struggling against the tide. "There's too many! They're too strong!"

"Robin!" I clutched the walkie-talkie. "We're stuck. We can't get away!"

"Don't worry, Master Jake!" Just hearing the robot's voice was reassuring. "The submarine should be with you at any moment."

I listened for the roar of the water dragon, waited for the shrieks of fear from the rustlers when they saw what was coming... But all I heard were the frightened complaints of the cows.

"Jake! I can see the lorry!" said Jess. "We're almost there!"

"Red Bull, we have a problem!" Robin

sounded worried. "I'm afraid the submarine is stuck in the mud."

"Well, they'd better get out quick!" said Jess. "Because we're about to get RUSTLED!"

DON'T PANIC!

"Don't worry, Master Jake, Miss Jess! I'm coming!"

"We're on the lorry!" I shouted into the walkie-talkie. There was no need to whisper now – the noise around us was deafening. "Maybe we should just get out of the costume and give ourselves up?"

"Don't be stupid!" said Jess. "You think they're just going to say, *Oh, sorry, we thought you were a cow. You go on home now. Our mistake!*"

"So what ARE we going to do?"

"Just be quiet for a minute and let me think!" Jess sounded more irritated than scared. In stressful situations, I tended to fall apart and freeze. When Jess felt threatened, she got angry – which often turned out to be much more useful. I'd never tell her, but I was glad my sister was here. "What we're NOT going to do," she told me, "is panic."

The walkie-talkie gave a squawk. "Master Jake! I'm ... motorbike ... come after you!" Robin's voice fizzed in and out, then faded.

The lorry gave an alarming shudder as doors slammed and the engine roared to life.

"We're moving!" I yelled into the radio.

"Don't wo..." said the robot, barely audible now. "I'm—" But the rest was swallowed by static, then silence.

"We must be out of range," said Jess.

Suddenly I felt very alone.

Robin wouldn't give up on us. His primary function was to keep me and Jess safe. Maybe THIS would finally make him see that we did still need a babysitter after all?

Then a horrible thought occurred to me. Grandma had reprogrammed the robot now he was living in the wild – what if we were no longer his number-one priority?

"You might as well take off the costume while we're stuck here," said Jess.

It felt good to stand upright again, but it was too dark in the back of the lorry to see much. The cows were packed all round us, like we were standing in a hairy sea. It reminded me of being in the crowd at the Metal Mayhem festival with Dad – minus the terrible music.

Something nudged me. When I turned round, one of the beasties was looking at me

too, huh?"
I scratched
her behind
the ear. "Don't
worry, there's
a tooled-up
robot coming
to rescue us."

The cow
licked my hand.

"Gross!" said Jess.

"She's hungry."

The beastie reminded me of Ali – *he* was
always hungry, although Ali didn't slobber quite
so much. I wondered what he was doing now.
Did Ali and Ivana even know we'd been rustled?
Would they even care?

I turned my attention back to the cow.

"As soon as Robin rescues us, you'll be back in your old field and you can eat as much grass as you like!"

Jess snorted, but I ignored her. I didn't feel quite so scared when I was talking to the beastie. Calming her down seemed to help me too!

I pictured the robot hunched over the handlebars of Granny Anderson's ancient motorbike, hot on our trail, and managed a smile. Robin would save us.

The lorry gave a sudden jerk and I noticed we were slowing down.

"Quick!" said Jess. "Join us back together!"

"I thought Robin would have caught up with us by now," I said, reattaching the two halves of the Spy Cow.

"He's probably keeping his distance so the rustlers don't know they're being followed, duh! Robin knows what he's doing."

She was right. The robot would have researched how to tail someone so he knew all the expert tricks. Robin would have the rescue planned down to the tiniest detail. He was just waiting for the right moment to leap into action.

I fastened the costume and, as the dark shut off my vision, it was like my hearing became ten times more powerful. I could hear my sister breathing, every snort and shuffle of the cows, even the distant croak of seagulls…

"Hey, Jess! Can you hear the sea?" It had to be my imagination, surely?

The lorry moved forwards again – slowly this time. There was a clang of metal and it felt like we were driving up some kind of ramp. The smell of oil suddenly filled my nostrils and I jumped when someone banged on the side of the lorry.

The engine died and for a moment an eerie

silence boomed in my ears. We heard voices outside and clanking footsteps fading into the distance. Then I realized that even though the lorry had stopped, we were still moving – no longer forwards but rolling gently from side to side, as though…

"We're on a BOAT!" It came out in a strangled squeak.

"I think you might be right," said Jess, which is when I knew something was badly wrong. My sister NEVER agrees with me.

A thunderous rumble rolled up from the depths. Then the boat began to throb and the rolling motion increased.

"We're moving!" I said. "Where are they taking us?"

"I don't know," Jess hissed. "Strangely enough, the captain didn't share the destination with me before we left."

I hated boats and this had to be a BIG

BOAT to fit a lorry on board. The kind of boat that went to SEA! There was a LOT of water in the sea and I DID NOT LIKE WATER!

Then something else occurred to me. "How's Robin going to rescue us if we're on a boat? Even he can't drive a motorbike across water!"

Jess didn't have an answer for that.

CHAPTER 10

NOW CAN I PANIC?

"I feel sick!"

"Don't you dare!"

It was the smell, the heat, the dark and the fear, but mostly it was the rolling motion. One minute the boat stuck its nose into the air like it was trying to take off, the next we were plummeting into an abyss. Just when I thought it was never going to end, we'd slam to a halt, tip backwards and the whole thing would start all over again.

"I don't know how much more I can take!"

From the sounds the cattle were making,
I guessed they were as scared as me. Which
also meant they were doing the things
creatures do when they're frightened. None of
which was helping my stomach.

I tried the walkie-talkie but it was dead.
I hoped Robin had seen the lorry drive on to
the boat, but even if he had what could he do?

"Now can I panic?" I asked Jess.

But my sister wasn't listening. "We're
slowing down!"

She was right. The boat had finally stopped
doing an impression of a rollercoaster.

"I think we've arrived," said Jess.

"Arrived where?" I'd be happy to get off the
boat, but what would be waiting when we did?

"We need to stay with the beasties and
hope the rustlers don't spot us," hissed
Jess. "Just act like a cow and DON'T SAY
ANYTHING!"

The lorry shuddered as the engine started up again and I felt the beastie nuzzle against me. I couldn't rub her ears now I was back inside the Spy Cow, but I told her we'd be OK and that I wouldn't let anything bad happen to her.

"Thanks," said Jess. "But why would I want you to rub my ears? In fact, if you come anywhere near my ears…"

This time we only drove a short distance before stopping again. We heard the rustlers get out.

"How long before the Big Man gets here?" said one.

"Och, he'll no be here before morning. We've time for a drink," his mate answered.

"We leavin' this lot here?"

"Unless you want to bring them up to the hoose, aye!"

"Right enough." Their laughter faded with

their footsteps as they walked away.

Around us the cows shuffled and stamped, breathing in nervous bursts.

"Now we find a way out of here," said Jess.

"I wonder who the Big Man is?" I said, climbing out of the cow costume. "How long is it until morning?"

"At least a few hours." My sister pointed to a narrow ventilation gap near the roof of the lorry. "We can get through there."

"You sure we'll fit?"

In answer, my sister scurried up and slipped out of sight like a letter through a postbox. I heard a thud as she hit the ground. "Jake! *Come on!*"

I'm rubbish at climbing, but I didn't want to be stuck in the lorry on my own. Sometimes fear allows you to do stuff that you wouldn't normally because the consequence of NOT doing it is even scarier!

It was a relief to be out of the lorry and breathing fresh air again. We were in a small harbour. I could see the boat we'd arrived on at the end of the quay. There were a few fishing boats tied up and a handful of old stone buildings, but everywhere was still in darkness.

The cows mooed sadly inside the lorry.

"We need to let the beasties out," I said.

Jess f.rowned. "We can't just *let them out*! What are we going to do with them then?"

It was a good point.

"We need to find a house or something," said Jess. "So we can phone Grandma – let her know where we are."

"But *we* don't even know where we are!"

"Come on," said Jess, ignoring me. "This way."

"Don't worry," I whispered to the beasties.

"We'll come back for you! I promise."

"JAKE! COME ON!"

I turned to follow my sister, then stopped. "Jess."

"What now?"

"If we were on an island, would that be good or bad?"

"What are you on about? Why would we be on an island?"

"Because this sign says *Welcome to Creel Island*." I pointed.

Jess stared at the sign.

"*Now* can I panic?" I asked.

CHAPTER 11

LEFT IS LUCKY
(USUALLY...)

"There's someone coming!" Jess grabbed my
arm. "This way, quick!"

We ran down the narrow street out of
the harbour, the sound of our feet loud in the
silence. "Where are we going?"

My sister didn't answer, just slipped into a
gap between two buildings where steep steps
led up into the darkness. They were uneven,
slippery and seemed to go on forever. I ignored
the burn in my legs and tried to keep up with
Jess who was racing ahead like a mountain goat.

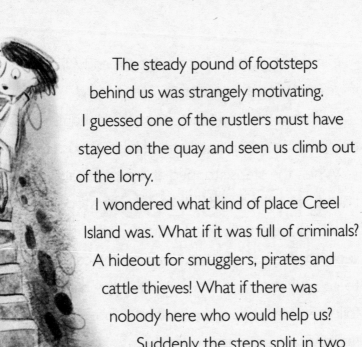

The steady pound of footsteps behind us was strangely motivating. I guessed one of the rustlers must have stayed on the quay and seen us climb out of the lorry.

I wondered what kind of place Creel Island was. What if it was full of criminals? A hideout for smugglers, pirates and cattle thieves! What if there was nobody here who would help us?

Suddenly the steps split in two directions and I realized I'd lost sight of Jess.

I listened but all I could hear was the steady thump of feet coming up the steps behind me. Whoever was chasing us was fit – they weren't even panting.

I had to keep moving.

If in doubt, go left. That's what me and Ali do if we're playing a video game. *Left is lucky!*

So I went left, and tried not to think about all the times that choice had ended badly for us.

When the steps stopped at a gate, I realized I'd chosen a dead end. I'd never understood why they were called that before — now it seemed chillingly obvious. I had no choice but to go back the way I'd come. If the guy had followed me, I was trapped. If he'd followed Jess, I would now be behind them ... but what was I going to do if I caught up with him?

There was a pile of firewood next to the gate, so I pulled out a chunky log. I wasn't sure what I was going to do with it, but it felt slightly better to have a weapon.

Slowly, I walked back the way I'd come, trying to stay quiet while my heart thumped loud enough to wake the entire island. Then I heard my sister cry out.

I ran towards the sound and saw two silhouettes up ahead. The guy had his back to me. If I stopped to think, I'd freeze. Before I had the chance, I raised the log over my head and brought it down on the man's back.

The sound it made was … unexpected. Hollow and slightly metallic.

My sister's attacker dropped to his knees so I hit him again. This time over the back of the head.

"JAKE! NO!" Jess grabbed my arm. "What are you DOING?"

"Rescuing you!" I hadn't expected gratitude and hugs, but this was a bit much even for her!

"IT'S ROBIN, YOU IDIOT!"

I stared in horror at the unconscious robot

lying at my feet. "What's HE doing here?"

"He came to rescue us! Duh!" said Jess.

"But … I mean … how did he even GET here?"

Jess kneeled down next to the robot. "I was about to ask when you ran up and hit him with a log. TWICE!"

"I thought he was attacking you!"

"He was hugging me!" My sister turned the robot over and his eyes snapped open.

"Master Jake! Miss Jess! How lovely to see you!"

"You're ALIVE!" I said.

"Technically, no," said Robin. "I am, however, operational."

"I'm sorry. I didn't mean to hit you over the head with a log."

"Twice!" said Jess.

We helped the robot to his feet.

"You were protecting your sister," he said. "The correct and logical response to the situation. You showed initiative and improvised – an essential skill for survival. Well done, Master Jake."

Jess folded her arms. "Excuse me! But I don't NEED protecting! I'm perfectly capable of looking after myself, thank you very much!"

"I won't bother next time then," I told her.

"Might I suggest we keep moving?" said the robot. "At the moment nobody knows we are here. Making our escape before that situation changes is highly desirable." He started back down the steps.

"How did you even get here?" I said, running to keep up.

"I gained access to the ship via the anchor chain," said the robot. "Unfortunately I got tangled up and was unable to free myself until we arrived and dropped anchor again."

"I told you me and Jess still need you to look after us!"

"On the contrary, Master Jake, you had already escaped by yourselves."

"Yeah, but we're still stuck on this island!"

"Which means that our next task is to find an adequate craft in which we can traverse the water back to the mainland."

"You mean we need to find a boat?" said Jess. "There were lots in the harbour."

"A BOAT!?" My voice came out in a horrified yelp. "There must be another way!"

"We're on an ISLAND, dummy!" My sister

shook her head. "So unless you've got a helicopter hidden up your t-shirt…"

"You want us to go to sea in THAT?" I looked at the tiny boat. It wasn't much bigger than our bath. "How do you know we can trust him?" The fisherman had been about to set off when Robin accosted him. He looked like a pirate – he even had a hook where his right hand should have been! "How do we know he's not one of them? Have you done some kind of robot-truth-scan thing?"

"No, but I agreed to exchange my multi-tool hand for his hook if he took us safely back to the mainland."

"Grandma won't be happy when she finds out you've given that away!" I said.

"I believe she will think it a cheap price to pay for the safe return of her grandchildren!"

I glanced back at the boat. Jess was already on board.

"We are only nine-point-six nautical miles from land," said Robin. "The tide will be in our favour so I estimate we should make landfall by daylight."

"That's when the Big Man's arriving!" I said. "What about the beasties? We can't just abandon them!"

"My priority is the safety of you and your sister, Master Jake," said the robot.

So Robin *was* still programmed to be our babysitter! Which meant there might still be a chance I could persuade him to come home with us. But first we had to get off this island and survive the trip.

The little boat was already bobbing around in the swell of the harbour.

"I hate boats!" I said.

"You'll be fine, Master Jake. I won't let anything bad happen to you."

Hadn't I promised the same thing to the beastie? "I'm not going without the cows!"

"Don't be stupid, Jake," said Jess. "How are we going to fit a load of beasties in here?"

"You go," I told her. "Call the police. Tell Granny Anderson. I'll wait here until they come and keep an eye on the cows." Then I turned and ran back up the slipway.

WHAT PLAN?

What was I DOING?

I wasn't sure if my main reason for running away was that I was too scared to get in the boat, or because I wanted to rescue the beasties – a bit of both probably.

Up close the lorry looked solid and un-break-into-able. There was a thick metal bolt with a hefty padlock between the cows and freedom.

I spotted a pile of rocks by a stone wall that was being repaired. It took all my strength to

lift one and drop it on to the padlock.
The beasties started mooing in alarm.

"Don't panic!" I told them. "I'm trying to
get you out."

I hefted the rock and tried again.

"Master Jake!" I'd guessed Robin would
come after me. "May I enquire as to your plan
once the cattle have been released?"

I paused. WHAT plan?

Then I noticed the big boat was still at the end of the quay, and had an idea.

"You know how you told us once that you could work a submarine?" I said.

The robot nodded. "I am programmed to operate over fifty different modes of transport, from a skateboard to an interplanetary orbiter."

"You'd be able to drive that boat then?"

"The correct term is *pilot*, but yes."

"And you could drive this lorry?"

Robin nodded and I felt the pieces of a plan falling into place.

"So … we hot-wire the lorry," I told him. "You drive it back on to that big boat. Then you dri— pilot the boat back to the mainland."

"An excellent plan, Master Jake. However, YOU will need to drive the lorry."

"ME? I can't drive!"

"On the contrary, I've seen you do it many

times in *Boy Racer Turbo Charged*."

"But that's a GAME! I've never driven a real car, let alone a lorry! You have to do it."

"I'm afraid that won't be possible."

"Why not? You just said you knew how to fly a spaceship! How hard can a lorry be?"

"Quite difficult when one has lost the use of one's legs. I suspect it may be a delayed reaction to being hit over the head with a log. Twice."

That explained why the robot hadn't moved since he'd caught up with me!

I was relying on Robin to get us out of this mess. How was he going to do that if his legs didn't work?

"Perhaps you could assist me to the lorry and we could drive together," Robin suggested. "You operate the pedals while I steer!"

Dragging a man-sized robot into the cab of a lorry isn't easy. Luckily, Robin's arms were still working, so he was able to haul himself up while I shoved from below.

"Please tell me that among your survival upgrades, there's one you can use to hot-wire a lorry?"

"Will this do?" asked Robin, holding up a key. "It was in the ignition."

Then I remembered something. "Where's Jess?"

Robin showed me his hand – or rather his *hook*. "On her way back to the mainland, I hope."

When Jess got back, she'd go to the police. But would they believe her? Even if they did, it could take ages! It was already starting to get light. Morning – and the Big Man – were coming. We didn't have time to wait for a rescue.

I looked round the cab. "OK, so what do I need to do?"

Who knew that REAL driving was so

complicated? Robin's instructions seemed to involve pressing and releasing various pedals *all at the same time*! To make things even harder, I could only reach the pedals by standing up. This was never going to work.

But it was all we had – our only chance. I reminded myself that Dad drove a lorry for his job – perhaps I'd inherited his skills?

"Excellent, Master Jake!" said the robot as we began to move. "Just ease back a little on the accelerator."

I lifted my foot and the lorry began to shudder.

"Not completely!" said Robin. "Or we'll stall."

I pressed down again and the lorry jerked forwards with renewed enthusiasm.

"When we reach the boat, you need to release the accelerator and step on the brake," he told me. "That's the pedal in the middle. You can press that one as hard as you like!"

I looked down to make sure I knew where the brake was. If I didn't press that, we'd drive right off the other side of the boat and into the sea, which would be—

"WATCH OUT!"

The man appeared from nowhere.

One minute the way to the boat was clear – the next a man in a high-vis jacket was in front of us, waving his arms.

I'm not entirely sure what happened next.

In my panic, I think I MIGHT have stamped down on the accelerator instead of the brake!

What I do know is that the lorry didn't stop.

There was a lot of noise, the smell of burning rubber and the feeling of being on a fairground ride as Robin wrestled with the steering wheel trying to:

a) not run over the guy in the high-vis jacket, and

b) not drive us over the edge of the quay into the sea.

But Robin is a robot and an excellent driver, so he managed both.

Sort of.

It seemed to happen in slow motion. I had time to think, *Oh, we seem to be heading towards the sea. I don't think we're going to stop in time. Yes, we're definitely going to end up in the water.*

But we didn't. Not quite.

CHAPTER 13

HANGING ON

When the world finally stopped spinning, we found ourselves tilting forwards at a steep angle – no longer on the quay but not in the water either. Instead, we were hanging in mid-air – as though somebody had pressed *pause* on a film.

I reached for the door handle, but Robin grabbed my arm. "Keep still, Master Jake!" he said. "We are in a very finely balanced position. It is only the weight of the cattle stopping us from tipping into the sea."

I stared at the deep black water churning below us and felt the lorry rocking like a see-saw.

The cows in the back were stamping with fear. Who was going to tell *them* to keep still?

"Master Jake," said the robot. "You're going to have to climb up the outside of the vehicle."

I stared at him. That bang on the head must have affected more than just his legs. What he wanted was impossible. Then something else occurred to me.

"What about you?"

The robot smiled. "Your safety is the most important thing, Master Jake. Unfortunately I am not functioning sufficiently to climb with you."

I shook my head. "I'm not going anywhere without you."

There was a shelf under the dashboard in the cab, crammed with old newspapers and cans. I spotted a coil of rope among the mess.

"Hang on! I've got a great idea," I told Robin. "We can use this to tie you to my back like a rucksack!"

"Ingenious, Master Jake! However, I'm afraid my added weight will make your climb much more difficult. I calculate that your chances of success will be greatly reduced with both of us."

"I don't care. I'm not leaving without you!"

Suddenly there was a loud crash from the rear of the lorry, followed by a scrambling of hooves.

"I fear your padlock demolition was more successful than we realized," said Robin.

I looked in the side mirror and saw the cows spilling out on to the quayside behind us. Then I remembered what Robin had said. "But, if all the cows get out, that means…"

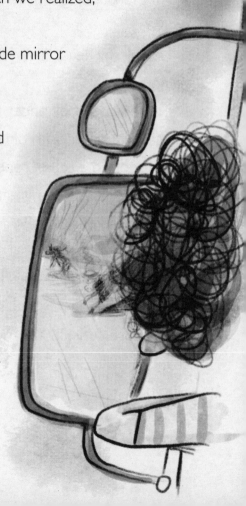

As the last beastie jumped down, the lorry dropped like a lift with its wires cut. The sea rushed towards us and I said something like, **"AAAAAAGGGGGGGHHHHH!"**

We stopped with a jolt – centimetres above the water.

"Our rear wheels must be caught on something," said the robot as a loud metallic groan rang through the air. "They will not hold us for long. You have to go now, Master Jake."

Icy water started seeping into the cab, each wave tugging at the lorry as if the sea itself was trying to suck us under.

Was this really how my eleven unremarkable years were going to end? At least I wouldn't have to go to Hardacre Academy now. It was strange though – starting Year Seven suddenly didn't seem that bad…

I didn't want this to be it. I had stuff to do. I hadn't got to the end of *Revenge of the*

Robots Two yet!

But the thing I wanted most was to get Robin home.

"Master Jake, your chances of survival are lowering with every—"

I held up a hand to shush the robot. "Grandma created you to look after me and Jess, right?"

"Yes. My primary function is to protect you."

"How are you going to do that if you get washed out to sea?"

The robot didn't answer.

"You need to survive so you can keep protecting me. Which means you have to come with me, or you will be failing your primary function." I couldn't believe I was trying to out-logic a robot!

"Your argument is very persuasive, Master Jake," said Robin.

"Good! So stop arguing and tie that rope

round your waist."

The water in the cab had risen to my knees.
It was now or never.

I pushed at the door and the sea rushed
in – all noise and spray and wind. I poked my
head out and squinted up. The lorry towered
above us, almost vertical now. I could see faces
peering down from the quayside. I guessed it
was the rustlers. Even if I managed to climb up,
they'd probably just throw us back in again.

"Can you see a handhold?" asked Robin
from over my shoulder.

The wooden struts on the side of the lorry
formed a kind of ladder. I took a deep breath
and started to climb.

It was even harder than I'd imagined. The
wood was wet and slippery. Robin felt like
a rucksack of bricks on my back, his weight
unpeeling my numb fingers from their fragile
hold. Waves crashed against the lorry below

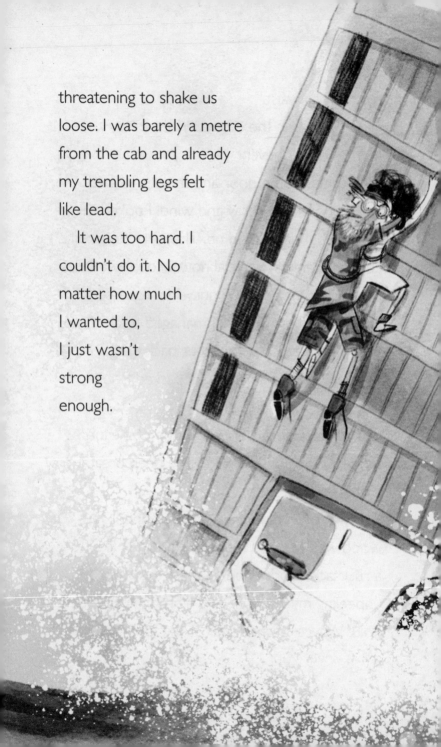

threatening to shake us
loose. I was barely a metre
from the cab and already
my trembling legs felt
like lead.

It was too hard. I
couldn't do it. No
matter how much
I wanted to,
I just wasn't
strong
enough.

"I'm going to untie the rope," said the robot.

"Without me you will make it."

"NO!" I shouted, but there was nothing I could do to stop him.

"Master Jake, my job is to protect you and in our current predicament this is the only way I can do that."

"But what about tomorrow and the day after? I NEED YOU!"

"No," said the robot gently. "YOU are all you need. You just have to believe in yourself the way you believe in me."

"Robin, PLEASE!" My face was wet, tears mixing with the spray.

I could feel him fumbling with the knot.

"Goodbye, Master Jake," said the robot. "It has been a privilege to know you and call you my friend."

CHAPTER 14

THE LAST HAUL

"WAIT!"

A rope thwacked against the side of the lorry. The figures hanging over the quay waved at me to grab it.

"DON'T LET GO!" I told Robin. "They've dropped us a rope!"

"May I suggest you grasp it as soon as possible?" said the robot.

I did.

Seconds later there was a horrible tearing sound as whatever was holding the lorry finally gave way. There was a splash as it hit the water and me and Robin found ourselves dangling in mid-air. The greasy rope started to slip through my fingers as our combined weight dragged me downwards.

"You have to climb, Master Jake!" said Robin.

"I CAN'T! I'm rubbish at climbing ropes!" I pictured myself dangling in the school gym while everyone laughed…

"Grip the rope between your knees," the robot told me. "Then pull yourself up – one hand over the other. You can do it."

But what if I couldn't?

Then Robin would untie himself and I'd lose him forever.

Suddenly I decided I was fed up of being laughed at. Fed up of being scared. I looked down at the rope and my flailing legs and somehow managed to twist them together.

We stopped sliding.

It worked!

Now, one hand over the other…

Slowly…

I started to climb.

I stood on the quay, my legs shaking, not quite believing we were back on dry land. There were beasties all over the harbour, the rustlers trying to round them up, but the cows weren't co-operating.

"The Big Man's no goin' tae be best pleased wi' youse two," said a weasel-faced guy throwing a blanket over us. He frowned at Robin, still roped to my back. "Wit's wrong wi' yer granda?"

I decided it would be best if they didn't find out that Robin was a robot. "Grandad hurt his legs in the crash," I said.

There was a shout from across the quay.

"This'll be the Big Man noo," said Weasel Face, marching us down the concrete slipway where two other rustlers were watching a grey shape approaching from the sea. "Wit the—?" Weasel Face squinted. "That disnae look like the Big Man's boot! That looks like…"

"A WATER DRAGON!" The woman standing next to him dropped her mug and started to run.

In the hazy dawn light, the bath-sub looked real and terrifying. A jet of flame spat from its jaws, making the air shiver with heat.

On the quay, beasties and rustlers bolted for cover. I waited for Weasel Face to let go of my arm, but he didn't. "That's no a water dragon!" he growled. "That's—"

Then we all heard the clack of a helicopter approaching. Was THIS the Big Man? Had our rescuers arrived too late?

"POLIS!" shouted Weasel Face and ran after his friends, leaving us alone on the slipway as the bath-sub coughed to a halt and the doors sprang open.

Digby was the first out, followed by Jess,
Ali and Ivana (on crutches). Granny Anderson
stuck her head out of the window and waved,
then Grandma popped up from the roof hatch.

"It's OK, you can thank me later," said Jess.
"How come you're all wet? Don't tell me you
fell in the sea again!"

"It's a long story," I told her, but it felt like
we were getting close to a happy ending.

THE END?

"What time's the train?" asked Ali for the third time.

"No doubt it will arrive when it gets here," said Granny Anderson.

"This holiday has gone too quickly!" Ivana sighed. "I can't believe we go back to school next week!"

"Year Seven," said Ali, looking worried.

"I'm sure you'll enjoy it once you settle in," said Grandma. "Make lots of new friends."

I didn't want new friends – I liked the ones

I had. But Ali was with Ivana now and Robin would be staying in Scotland.

I'd thought that if we caught the rustlers Robin would come home, but the robot said that Granny Anderson still needed his help.

"Your great-grandma's systems are not as operational as they once were," he'd told me. "I can be of assistance to her. You and Miss Jess have grown up – you no longer need a babysitter."

Now I thought about it, me and Jess were different from the people who ran out of school and saw the robot that first time. The old version of me had been disappointed with Robin. We'd even plotted to get rid of him! It was hard to believe we'd ever felt like that now. I was glad we'd changed!

Some of the stuff we'd done – rescuing Robin; rebuilding him; solving a mystery and fighting a robot army; getting rustled and saving the beasties – the old Jake couldn't have done any of those things, but I had.

"You'll still be my mate, won't you?" Ali whispered.

"What?"

"When we go to Big School. Promise you'll still be my best mate!"

"Of course. But what about Ivana?"

Ali frowned. "She's my girlfriend. You're still my best mate!"

We grinned at each other.

"Hey! I can see the train!" Jess pointed down the track.

"This is a request stop," said Granny Anderson. "You have to stick your arm oot."

"I'll do it," said Robin.

I'm not sure exactly what happened. Maybe the robot forgot that he had a hook for a hand and stood a little too close to the edge? But the next thing we knew, Robin was attached

to the train, running along the platform,
hurdling our bags as he went.

Ali filmed it on his phone and we watched it on the way home until we were all crying with laughter – at least that's what we said it was.

We were going to miss our robot babysitter, but, after everything we'd been through together, it felt like Robin was still there with us. He probably always would be.